T0157024

ABRAHAM:

THE FAITH CHILD

DANIEL E. LEVISTON

iUniverse, Inc.
Bloomington

Abraham
The Faith Child

This is a work of fiction. All of the characters, names, incidents, organizations, and dialogue in this novel are either the products of the author's imagination or are used fictitiously.

iUniverse books may be ordered through booksellers or by contacting:

iUniverse
1663 Liberty Drive
Bloomington, IN 47403
www.iuniverse.com
1-800-Authors (1-800-288-4677)

Because of the dynamic nature of the Internet, any web addresses or links contained in this book may have changed since publication and may no longer be valid. The views expressed in this work are solely those of the author and do not necessarily reflect the views of the publisher, and the publisher hereby disclaims any responsibility for them.

Any people depicted in stock imagery provided by Thinkstock are models, and such images are being used for illustrative purposes only.

Certain stock imagery © Thinkstock.

ISBN: 978-1-4620-3375-1 (sc)
ISBN: 978-1-4620-3376-8 (e)

Printed in the United States of America

iUniverse rev. date: 8/23/2011

Acknowledgments

Unless otherwise indicated, all Scripture quotations were taken from The Holy Bible Authorized King James Version, Kenneth Copeland Reference Edition. Used by permission.

I would like to grant a special thanks to Rena for your support and painstaking editing of this project.
Your acts of kindness will never be forgotten.

Author's Note

Not to belittle Abraham, the father of many nations (Genesis 17), but I purposely chose his name because he was, according to God, strong in faith (Romans 4:20). Although this is a fictional story, I am convinced that, with God's help, it could very well become a reality. To all who read this book, I pray that you are encouraged to trust the Lord even more so. If by any chance you find yourself portrayed by Abraham, I know that you will be blessed. If this portrayal happens to come during a negative time in your life, do not stop reading—do not give up—because you will see that weeping may endure for a night, but joy definitely comes in the morning. If reading this book happens to come during a positive time in your life, do not get high minded. Thank God for his grace. Again, I want to reiterate that this story is fictional. If any single person is portrayed without his or her permission, it is strictly coincidental.

CONTENTS

INTRODUCTION

M y name is Maurice Evans, and I'm a freelance writer who specializes in writing biographies. I have always loved reading—for as long as I can remember—but, for some reason, I found early on that biographies especially sparked my interest. That was fine and well, but the problem was that if I had to discuss what I read, I would become terrified because I stuttered. Now, I didn't stutter every time I spoke; I learned that, when I became excited, that's when I stuttered the most. As strange as this may sound, reading challenges and triumphs that people experienced in various biographies sure excited me. I have been told most of my life that I will always stutter, and there is nothing I can do to change it. So I learned how to manage this problem over the years, but I still felt cheated because I couldn't enjoy the excitement of different things in my life as I wanted to. To my surprise, this would soon change.

I was in my home office one day when a friend arrived. He helped by doing research for my books when needed, and he had heard about a very old religious fanatic.

"What did you s-s-say?" I asked. "Did I-I-I hear you-you-you co-co-correctly?" Excitement overwhelmed me.

"Calm down," Chester responded. "Yes, you heard correctly. There is an old man who is very, very religious living somewhere in Iowa. You might be interested in knowing more about him. I have to go, but here is a number you can call to get in contact with him."

After Chester left, I thought about what he'd said. I'm not as religious as others, but I do know something about God and prayer. Is it possible that this old religious fanatic may have some idea about how I might be able to get rid of this stutter?

I found out that the man was living in Jordan, Iowa. He was over 110 years old, and I just had to pen his life story. After leaving messages and making numerous attempts by telephone, I finally was able to catch up with Mr. Abraham Caldwell. He was just as active as someone far younger.

"M-M-Mister Caldwell," I said. "My n-n-name is Maurice Evans. After hearing a-about you (especially your age), w-w-well, it sparked my interest. I-I-I would like, with your permission, to wr-wr-write your life story."

With a puzzled look, Mr. Caldwell asked, "Why the stuttering? Are you nervous?"

"No," I responded. "I have been stuttering most of my life, but for some reason, it only happens when I get very excited."

Mr. Caldwell replied, "Tell me quickly, Mr. Evans. Why should I let you write my story? After all, I have been approached by some of the largest publishing companies, and they offered a lot of money. I turned them all down. Why should I say yes to you?"

"Well, M-M-Mister Caldwell. I know, like everyone else, that you are a lawyer, preacher, and philanthropist, but I also know that you are a man of gr-gr-great wisdom. From what I have heard, your wisdom does not come from life, but from God, the giver of life. This is the element I w-w-want and believe you want portrayed in your story."

"Enough said," replied Abraham. "Mr. Evans, you have the job, but do try not to get too excited. Also, Mr. Evans, I did not say yes because of your answer, which was pretty good. From the first time you called, I asked and received confirmation from the Lord that you are the one I should let write my story. Excuse me for a moment as I forward a message to my office." Mr. Caldwell adjusted his watch and told it to send a message to his office that he and I were to start meeting together for several interviews. "Oh, by the way, if we are going to pursue this project, I insist that you call me Abraham. I know it may take some adjustment on your part, but I would not allow you to write this book if I couldn't call you friend—and all my friends call me Abraham. Do you have a problem with that?"

"No-no-no-no, Mr.Caldwell—I mean Abraham. No problem at all."

A few days later, I was sitting across from Abraham "The Faith Child" Caldwell.

As I listened, I could not help (not that I objected) noticing the sincerity in his eyes as he unfolded his life's story before me. He was in what he called divine health.

"Is that possible?" I asked.

"Without a doubt. But don't take my word for it. With God as my witness, every word I'm about to say to the best of my knowledge is true."

It was the summer of 2064, and we were enjoying a cool breeze blowing off a lake that was close to his property. This was the first of many interviews. I was anticipating more than it actually took because I wanted to give Abraham the liberty to take as much time as he needed.

"Let's see … where was I? Oh, yes," he said as he adjusted himself in his chair. "You wanted to know about my divine health. First, I will have you know that I was an only child, so some of the things children with a brother or sister might get away with, I wasn't able to. My parents were what some may call fanatics when it came to spiritual things—so much so that it had a very, very strong influence on my life even before I was born."

I began to wonder if Abraham knew that some people thought that he was a religious fanatic as well.

"My father, a publisher, and mother, a schoolteacher, were adamant about reading, writing, and everything else as far as education goes. During Mom's pregnancy, she would keep journals describing the changes her body went through—about how she felt at different times and how I responded to different things at different stages of her pregnancy. These journals were documented and preserved because, as the years went by, Dad and Mom penned numerous pages. These became sentimental treasures to our family."

Abraham would periodically refer to the journals which he had scanned and downloaded on an iPad (which he treasured almost as much as the Bible itself). For the most part, everything he told me was from memory. In the quiet town of Jordan, Iowa, I found out why Abraham truly deserved to be called "The Faith Child."

BEFORE BIRTH

"Hi, Abraham. Mommy loves you. You are very special. I am so glad the Lord has given you to us. Daddy says hi also. He loves you just as much as I do. That is exciting, huh? Well, guess what? Jesus loves you more than Mommy does and Daddy ever could. Listen to this:

> For God so loved the world, that He gave his only begotten Son, that whosoever believeth in him should not perish, but have everlasting life (John 3:16).

"That is one of many conversations my parents had with me before I was born. Wait, I'm getting ahead of myself. I am the fruit of what some may call extremely planned pregnancy. You see, my parents loved God and His Word. They not only believed it—they practiced it literally. They found out the truth in the scripture where it says:

> Moreover, Jesus answering saith unto them, have faith in God. For verily I say unto you, that whosoever shall say unto this mountain be thou removed and be thou cast into the sea; and shall not doubt in his heart, but shall believe that those things which he saith shall come to pass: he shall have whatsoever he saith. Therefore, I say unto you, what things so ever you desire when you pray, believe that you receive them and you shall have them (St. Mark 11:23 and 24).

1

"Knowing this—and taken with that—another scripture reads:

> Verily I say unto you, whatsoever you shall bind on earth shall be bound in heaven: and whatsoever you shall loose on earth shall be loosed in heaven. Again I say unto you, That if two of you shall agree on earth as touching anything that they shall ask, it shall be done for them of my Father which is in heaven (Matthew 18:18–19).

"In their hearts, they believed, joined hands, and prayed according to God's word that they would receive a male child with hazel eyes and red hair—even though they both had blue eyes and blond hair. They prayed before coming together and being intimate with each other. For the whole nine months, everything they did agreed with the confession they made when they prayed. Whenever they referred to me, it was in the male gender. They only bought boy's clothes. She would ask my father if he wanted to feel him move or tell him to put his hand on her stomach to feel how hard he can kick.

"They would not let anyone—not even the doctors—refer to me as anyone other than him or he. My parents even gave me my name before I was born as an act of their faith. I was told—as the journals testify—that even before Mother became pregnant with me, some of the most unusual things happened. This could be directly blamed as an attempt to get my parents to doubt God's word even the least bit. Mother had such a difficult time becoming pregnant that the doctors and others thought that perhaps it was not possible and they should just give up trying. Mother was not feeling one hundred percent during her pregnancy—especially during the last trimester—and had a fever she could not get rid of.

Between the fever and Father's demanding work schedule, they were not able to fellowship with other believers as much as they would have liked. Their faith in God was really being tested. If that wasn't enough, the big test came when they heard that a couple who were very strong in their faith walk with the Lord—seasoned Christians, you might say—had a baby about three months before I was due. As much as they believed and confessed their belief around Mom and Dad for a healthy baby, their baby was born with Down's syndrome.

"You can imagine what that could have done to my parents' faith since they didn't consider themselves to be on the same faith level as the other couple. Nevertheless, they continued to believe God. In spite of how things looked, a male child with hazel eyes and red hair was born to them. I was healthy and came out without any major complications—even though Mother never did fully get rid of that fever until I was born. My birth had a big impact on the development of their faith in God and His word. To believe for something and not have someone to look at as an example of having done that exact thing before will definitely expand your faith—especially when it is manifested right before your eyes."

CHILDHOOD

From the time Abraham was born, he was better known as "The Faith Child." Even though it's already stated that Susan had declared boldly from the first time she and Robert prayed that this child would be male, restating it stresses how **powerful** their initial act of faith really was. So, during the rest of her hospital visit and as she was leaving to take Abraham home for the first time, whenever someone saw her, they would say, "Here comes Susan and her faith child."

"Most were saying it joyfully, and some were being sarcastic, but Mom didn't mind because she knew that their faith in God had produced exactly what they wanted.

"Being called a faith child was not an easy pill to swallow. Looking back, in my opinion, I really believe I had to use my faith far more than anyone else—even though I can't prove it. For my parents, sure, it was a great testimony, but for me … oh, let me tell you. From the time I can remember to their last days on earth, my parents instilled in me to say what I wanted to happen. They would not let me be comfortable speaking any other way. That is good while you are small, at home, and around them most of the time. But, when you get older and go to school without them, things can become quite interesting. When I was very young, probably seven or eight, a boy at school was picking at me because of my nickname. I didn't fully understand at that time what *faith child* or even the word *faith* meant, and neither did he, but he had heard that it had something to do with the phrase 'What you believe is what is supposed to happen.'

"Jesus actually said, 'Therefore I say unto you what things so ever you

5

desire when you pray believe that you receive them and you shall have them' (Mark 11:24).

"I can remember as if it were yesterday," Abraham said with a smile. "Hey Faith Child, Faith Child, Faith Child. Do you believe if I hit you, it wouldn't hurt?' he asked.

"I ignored him, of course, but that only agitated him and caused him to become more forceful. 'Hey Faith Child, Faith Child, Faith Child, didn't you hear what I said? If I hit you, do you believe it wouldn't hurt?' He swung and hit me so hard (I had never been hit that hard before) that I started crying and swinging at once. When the teachers got there to separate us (other children had gathered around chanting), we were both bruised, had torn clothes, and were sent home for the rest of the day. After that incident, I remember two things happening. First, my father punished me for fighting; and second, both he and Mom sat me down and explained what faith child meant to them and why they chose to make it part of my name. I don't know if I fully understood at that time, but I remember trying my best from then until now not to be offended if anyone else yelled 'Hey Faith Child' sarcastically.

"One of my favorite pastimes is reading. I have enjoyed reading as far back as I can remember. Where the love for reading came from ... I don't know? Yeah right. Of course I know that it came from my parents reading to me all the time. Plus, there were books always around the house. I don't care what it was—adventure, autobiographies, sports, science, romance, and even inspirational—if it was near and I hadn't read it, I was going to read it the first chance I got. Whenever my parents had something for me to do or somewhere for me to go and could not find me, they knew I would be somewhere with a book in my hand.

"Maurice, as you can guess, the school and public libraries became my favorite places to go. I grew up in a house that had a basement and an attic, so you can imagine if a little boy wanted to disappear for a while, finding somewhere to go was always available.

"'Abraham, Abraham, where are you? Do not make me come and get you,' Mother yelled. 'Oh there you are. What were you doing—as if I need to ask? Oh, I know, reading a book?' 'Oh yes, Mom, and it is good. It is about this little boy who is looking for treasure and he is captured by pirates.' 'Well, that's good and dandy, but I need you to go to the store for me and pick up some things.' 'Aw, do I have to?' 'Yes, and do not make any detours. Go there and come right back because I need some of the seasonings to prepare dinner.' 'Okay," I said, and off to the store I went.

"Getting the things Mother wanted from the store was no problem, but while I was on my way back home, I passed the library. I could see Mrs. Wilberson standing by the window. She waved as I passed. Now, this was a Saturday evening and the library was usually closed at this hour. So when I saw Mrs. Wilberson, I decided to stop in for a moment. 'Good evening, Mrs. Wilberson, how are you doing? Why is the library still open? Did you get some new books in? I bet you did.' 'Hold on. Slow down, Abraham. I'm doing fine and thanks for asking. I got a call that some new books were being delivered to answer your second and third questions. So I came down right away to open the door for the delivery man.' 'Well, are there any I would like?' 'I don't know, I haven't had a chance to look at all of them but, out of the books I saw, there was only one I think might be for your age and I think you would be interested in. Let me see, what did I do with it? Oh, here it is. *Jesus Christ: His Childhood Years.*'

"When I saw the cover, my eyes got as big as saucers. I sat down and forgot about everything and everybody else around me. I went to church and Sunday school—boy did I, my parents saw to that—and I had heard the story of Jesus being born in a manger and dying on the cross and other things he did as an adult, but I had never heard about him being a little boy. When I opened the pages and started finding out that Jesus cried just as I did when he scraped his knee while playing, and he was made to eat vegetables, especially the ones he didn't like, and he went to school even though he may not have felt like going all the time or that he played with other kids who sometimes thought he was strange but did not know why.

"I completely forgot all about the time until my father yelled, '*Abraham, my faith child, what are you doing in this library?*' He was standing right over me. I think he said my 'faith child' to keep himself from doing something he would later regret. He grabbed my ear with one hand, the groceries with the other, made me leave the book, said good-bye to Mrs. Wilberson, and walked with me that way all the way home. For three blocks, he explained the meaning of being responsible and considerate of others. My punishment for that act was being made to sit in the living room with my parents after supper without saying a word. As soon as it got dark, I was sent immediately to my bedroom, instructed to turn the lights off as soon as I was ready for bed, and not to turn them on again. I wasn't able to read in bed before I went to sleep—and my parents knew that would hurt me more than any other type of punishment.

"I was an average child in most ways except during conversations. I learned at an early age what was—and what was not—allowed to come out of my mouth. Using vulgar language was a definite no-no. My parents also did not allow me to say negative confessions: I always get a cold when it's cold outside or math is always going to be a hard class for me no matter who the teacher is, for example. That made a drastic change throughout my life and I learned to appreciate it wholeheartedly—even up to this day.

"I was involved in church activities like going to children's church, youth groups, and the youth choir. I went to school, movies, on hikes, field trips, played sports, and even went on a few dates—nothing serious, though. Boy did I like sports—all sports—almost as much as reading. I quickly learned that I wasn't good at all of them so I concentrated my efforts on the ones I was best at: basketball and baseball. My ability to play basketball and baseball was so good that I was invited to play on my varsity teams at school from ninth grade through senior year.

"An incident in the middle of my junior year of high school got me kicked off both the baseball and basketball teams the rest of that year and, if it had been my senior year, I probably would have lost my college scholarship. What started out as a prank—ended up being far more serious than I ever thought. One evening while football practice was still in session, some of us who had finished practice early decided to let all of the air out of the tires on the principal's car. Of course, after the police were involved, many questions were asked and some soul-searching was done on our part. Realizing that confession was good for the soul, we decided to do just that and receive the punishment we definitely deserved. I thought the suspension and being kicked off the teams was tough, but those could not compare with what my parents did. To say they were disappointed would be an understatement. They were shocked with disbelief and hurt most of all.

"'Abraham, of all things, how could you get involved in such a stunt? Were you not thinking at all?' Well, to make sure I understood just how serious what I did was and most of all not to follow the crowd, every ounce of freedom I had was revoked for the rest of that year. That meant no television, driving, hanging out with friends, going to concerts, conferences, or anything that remotely resembled extracurricular activities. Of course, I thought the punishment was too severe for the crime, but getting my parents to change their minds was out of the question. For the rest of the year, since no non-educational activities were allowed, I spent all of my free time reading. You would think that, after being in school most of the day, I would be tired of looking at books. I was tired of looking at textbooks, but they were nothing like a good adventure.

"One thing I noticed was that all of the books I chose to read dealt with the law in some form or another. Sure, I enjoyed reading science fiction, sports, autobiographies, or even horror, but even in venturing out in these areas, I always seemed to get a book that had a law overtone. A good detective mystery like Sherlock Holmes or a courtroom adventure such as Perry Mason would spark my interest every time. I came to the conclusion that I enjoyed—and began to understand—how the law affects everyone in our community and everywhere else. I was intrigued by how lawyers use the law to get a desired result. I noticed that—even though I still loved sports—my desire to participate in them to the same extent was diminishing. I still wanted to participate in high school and perhaps college, but I wanted to be able to help people become better than they may have thought possible. If it is possible to say that one thing helped me decide what I probably wanted to do in life, it was when I came across a book about *Brown v. the Board of Education*. It told the story of how some people were mistreated for a long time and because of the way a lawyer defended them, they were able to receive their rightful reward.

"I was a senior in high school and was positive that I wanted to pursue a law degree. I had to choose which college was best suited for me. My grades were exceptional—so that wasn't a problem—and I even had a few scholarship offers to play baseball, but I just could not pick one. Mom and Dad suggested that I pick a school close to home so that they would see me more and the tuition wouldn't be so expensive.

"As the deadline for sending out college applications approached, Dad noticed that I hadn't made a decision. He said, 'Son, I know this is a tough decision for you, but don't let what Mother and I want pressure you. Choose the college that is in your heart. Abraham, if you still cannot pick one, remember what you have been taught. Go to God and ask him which school is best for you—it will probably be one of the colleges in the group you want anyway.'

> Trust in the Lord with all thine heart and lean not unto thine own understanding. In all thy ways acknowledge him, and he shall direct thy paths (Proverbs 3:5–6).

"Before I got into bed, I asked God to show me which college was best for me. And as you know, I went to Harvard. You want to know something, Maurice? That's the real reason I went to Harvard. Some people think I went because it is a big name school and they offered me a baseball scholarship, but I really wanted to go to the University of Iowa. It was closer to home, was a big name school, and they also offered me a scholarship. You may find this hard to believe—even though I was a senior and getting ready to go to college—I was still a child at heart. I wanted to stay at home in that small country town near Mom and Dad as long as possible. I knew that once I left home, things would never be the same. I guess that is all part of growing up and becoming an adult."

College Years

In our second interview, contrary to what people may have expected, I got the impression that Abraham was comfortable talking about his life. With a life as rich as his, who would not be eager to tell it? I guess, as with our own lives, Abraham may have wished that he had done some things differently.

"Good morning, Abraham. Did you get a good night's rest?"

"Yes I did. Good morning to you, Maurice. I trust all is well with you this beautiful morning? Before we get started, I have something to tell you. After you left yesterday, I spent some quality time with the Lord. You and your stuttering were impressed in my spirit. Do you mind if I pray with you, Maurice?"

"Why, s-s-sure you c-c-can. P-p-please do before I become excited."

"Before I pray, Maurice, I believe with all my heart that God's word is true and He will do exactly what he said:

> And these signs shall follow them that believe in My name … they shall lay hands on the sick and they shall recover (Mark 16:17–18).

"Maurice, stuttering is a type of sickness. I believe that when I lay hands on you and pray, God will do the healing. So let's pray. Heavenly Father, in the powerful name of Jesus we come giving you praise as our healer because you alone are worthy of that honor. Right now, as I lay hands on Maurice, I thank you for your healing power flowing through him and correcting whatever problem is causing him to stutter. I thank you—from this moment forward, he is totally healed. In Jesus's name, we pray. Amen. Now, Maurice, all you have to do is believe and confess what God has done and the manifestation will follow if you faint not in your faith. Now, are you ready to continue with the interview?"

"Yes, I am."

"Those college years were nothing like what I thought they would be. From the very first day, far from home and with more freedom than I could imagine, I was overwhelmed. The adjustment of going to classes on time—some early in the morning and others later in the evening—doing homework, studying, and preparing for exams wasn't a problem. The problem was what to do after school when I didn't have any evening or weekend classes. There wasn't anyone there to tell me how late to stay out, where not to go, or who not to hang out with. Some people were easy to figure out because of their lifestyle. I knew not to hang out with them and I knew some places to avoid because of my lifestyle. Other people were not so easy to figure out. That is where Brad Redman came into the picture—or into my life, if you will. Brad Redman was a freshman, played on the baseball team, and was smart in the classroom. We were drawn to each other like peas in a pod. Oh, I didn't mention I was on the baseball team? Sorry, I don't see how I let that go unmentioned. I did get a baseball scholarship after all. Yes, I was on the baseball team and was good, I must say, but it didn't turn into a career.

"We had a lot in common, but one area that we were different was in conversing with people of the opposite sex. Brad, like me, was from a small town, but his experience with women was light years from mine, at least according to what he told me. You know, Maurice, young men tend to embellish when telling stories about themselves and women, but I do suspect some of the things Brad told me were true. Brad 'the talker' and Abraham 'the quiet guy' is how some of the young women in our classes described us. Being around Brad helped my confidence and it helped me feel more comfortable while talking and being in the presence of young women altogether.

"In the middle of my freshman year, one young woman by the name of Valarie Cummings caught my fancy. It happened at a victory party after one of our baseball games. Since the party was on campus and no alcohol was allowed, I decided to attend. I remember that moment as if it was yesterday—even though that was quite some time ago. I guess various events caused us to cross paths. I was getting something to drink when I saw a woman I had never seen before. She wasn't in any of my classes—and didn't attend any of the baseball games as far as I knew. I had never seen her in the library, or anywhere else on campus, in fact. She was the tallest—she was almost as tall as me and I am six foot five—and prettiest woman I had ever seen. When Brad passed by, I grabbed him by the arm and asked, 'Who is that young woman by the door? I have to meet her.' Brad smiled and said, "Oh, that's Valarie. Just walk up to her and introduce yourself.' 'I can't do that. Suppose something weird happens.' 'Okay, come on.'

"He introduced us. I was about to tell her my name when she said, 'Abraham. Abraham Caldwell. I know who you are. You're the shortstop, number 8 on the baseball team.' I asked, "How do you know who I am? I don't recall seeing you before.' 'That's because I am not a student here. I am a senior in high school and Brad invited me to the party.' 'Brad, how long have you known Valarie?' 'Oh, for about two months. We met at the Trebek. It's a local hangout.'

"Valarie and I spent the rest of the evening talking and getting to know more about each other. She had been to some of our games, but I had never seen her—even as tall as she is. When it was time to leave, we exchanged phone numbers and I knew right away that I was smitten. For the next twelve months, Valarie and I were inseparable. We learned a lot about each other. I found out she was the oldest of four kids. Her parents were active in their children's lives. She planned to go to college, become a teacher, get married, and raise a family of at least two children. First, she wanted to graduate from high school and enjoy herself a little before starting college.

"I told Valarie about myself, how I enjoyed school and playing baseball, and I aspired to become a lawyer. Valarie liked that my mom was a teacher; maybe she could give her some advice. Valarie was the first person I told since I'd left for college that I was known at home as the Faith Child. She asked what it meant. I explained that my relationship with the Lord was very special. To my family, it was more than religion. Since what God says in the Bible is exactly what he means, we talk and act accordingly. I explained how my parents had asked for a child like me and why I was called the Faith Child.

Therefore, I say unto you, what things so ever ye desire when ye pray, believe that ye receive them, and ye shall have them (Mark 11:24).

"'Wow,' said Valarie. 'Even though I'm a Christian and I love the Lord, I have never heard anyone talk about God like that before.'

"When I first took Valarie to meet my parents, it was wonderful—they were all excited. I had bragged about their strong faith in God. That was new to her, and she wanted to see it in action. My parents were excited because of all the things I had told them. They could tell I was in love with her and perhaps she was the one. They fell in love with her right away, and she with them. My parents were amazed at her quick wit and loved the fact that she could converse about various topics, including religion. They thought that if I got involved with someone who was raised in a larger family, perhaps I would gain a greater understanding of what they had tried to do, and see the advantages of being an only child.

"'Your parents can find God in any conversation and I love it. I believe if they asked God for an auditorium for us to have our wedding or when we get married, they would think He would give it to them. You know what? He probably would. They told me how their faith in God made a difference. Your mom once misplaced her car keys and they turned the house inside out, but the keys were nowhere to be found. She said, "The Holy Spirit is our helper—let's ask him to show us where the keys are." In less than five minutes, the Holy Spirit told her to go look in the car. They were on the seat where she had dropped them the night before.'

"'You know what, Valarie? You're right about the auditorium. The things my parents have believed God for over the years are amazing. One time, my father was taking me to a publisher's conference and the engine in our old Chevy started hesitating like it wanted to stop. Mom was not able to go because she was grading exams for the classes she had the next day. Dad pulled off the road, cut the engine, and said, "Son, let's pray. Heavenly Father, I do not have extra money to have this car towed and pay a repair bill. Please send someone who can fix our car and not charge us a dime. Thank you for it already being done in Jesus's name. Amen. Now, son, just watch and see what God does."

"I asked, 'Do you think someone will come?' He said, 'Just have faith.'

Almost right at that moment, a man in a tow truck pulled up behind us, introduced himself, and asked what the problem was. The driver looked under the hood and informed us that the alternator needed to be replaced, but we shouldn't worry, he had a spare one that he thought would fit. He'd brought it from his shop to put on another car, but they didn't need it. Dad whispered, 'God had him bring it for us.' Not long after Dad whispered, the driver closed the hood and told him to see what it would do. Dad turned the key and our car started right up. When the car was running, the man jumped in his truck and said, 'Don't worry about the charge. Put it in church when you get a chance and y'all have a nice trip.'

"Wait a minute, Abraham. How can you remember that far back in such detail?"

"Well, Maurice, it's not so much as what happened that helps me remember, it's what Dad told me after the truck driver left. He said, 'Son, if you are doing exactly what God tells you to do and you are doing it exactly when he tells you to do it, then he will make sure you have everything you need.' That, Maurice, is a saying I have remembered and have been living by from that moment until now."

"So, Abraham, how did you learn how to know what God wanted you to do and when?"

"Maurice, that is something I'll have to tell you at a later time. Now let me get back to my story. Valarie told me that was the most amazing story she had ever heard and that, after being with my parents that evening, she didn't doubt it. Valarie graduated from high school and joined me at Harvard where she pursued an education degree, but she later changed to the pursuit of a law degree. As time passed, Valarie and my mom became really close (that was because I was either talking about Valarie every time I called home or bringing her with me). She slept in the extra bedroom, of course. During those visits, Valarie's relationship with the Lord became stronger, and she actually saw my parents' faith in action.

"There is one thing in particular I would say that had a big impact on Valarie fully understanding the difference between just being religious and having a relationship with Jesus Christ. I was a senior at Harvard, and my family was going through a very difficult time." Abraham looked at me, and I could see his facial expression change from serious to hurt.

It looked as if what he was getting ready to tell me was too painful and hard to mention.

"Abraham, if what you are going to tell me is too painful, you do not have to relive it; we can leave it out of the book."

"Yes, Maurice. It is painful and does hurt to relive, but I must tell it because I know someone will be blessed by reading this. During my senior year at Harvard, one evening after baseball practice, I received a call from home. Mom said there had been an accident, and I needed to come home immediately.

"After talking with Mother, I called Valarie and told her what Mother said and that I was going home and didn't know when I would be back. Because of the seriousness of our relationship, she decided to leave school as well. I persuaded Valarie that leaving school would not be in her best interest and would be a big waste of money since she would have the extra expense of a hotel. She suggested that she could sleep in the extra bedroom. I reminded her that both Mom and myself would not be at home at the same time, and her being there with me alone would not reflect a Christian lifestyle. She agreed and stayed in school.

"On the way home, I prayed for the strength to be able to face whatever challenge came before me. As I got closer, I became confident that God would answer my prayer. Had I not prayed, I know without a doubt that I would not have been able to handle what I saw. Mom met me at the door, and she looked like she had been crying from the time I talked with her on the phone up to this moment.

"She said, 'Abraham, your father has been in a very terrible car accident.'

"'How is he?' I asked.

"'Oh, he is stable and God is able,' she replied.

"Mom squeezed in the car and we drove straight to the hospital without removing any luggage.

"'What happened?' I asked.

"'The driver in an approaching vehicle fell asleep at the wheel and drifted into your father's lane. It was a head-on collision. The police officers, doctors, and some others who heard about the details of the accident said Robert was lucky to be alive, but I know without a doubt it is because of God's grace and mercy that he is alive.'

"'Mom,' I said, 'I know God is in control, but why did this have to happen in the first place and for what purpose?'

"'Abraham, why this happened and for what purpose, I don't know, but I do know that God is the same yesterday, today, and forever more, and his love for us never changes. That is what I believe now and have always believed. Just because something bad happens in our lives—that is not the time to stop believing in what has carried you through. Besides, I don't have anything else to believe, especially now.'

"'Mother, you are amazing. I know you and Dad have been trusting God for quite some time, but to have that kind of faith in God with what just happened is not normal. It's hard for me to really understand how you can continually do it.'

"'It's not me, honey, that's amazing. It's the God in me who is amazing. Without Him, I would be a total basket case. I am feeling hurt, angry, lonely, and flabbergasted, but reacting to those feelings wouldn't help solve anything. As much as I would like to, I can't allow the devil to win by reacting to how I feel. I can speak what I believe again and again—no matter how long it takes—until I start feeling what I believe more than what I see.'

"While we were pulling into the hospital parking lot, Mother looked at me and said, 'Your father is heavily sedated and probably will not know we are there, but we are not to be too alarmed by what we see.'

"When I walked in the hospital room and saw Dad, I thanked Mom for preparing me, and God for giving me the strength to handle what I saw. When I first saw Dad hooked up to all those tubes and machines, I almost fainted. I looked over at Mom, and the peace on her face was all it took for me to gather my composure and say something to Dad. I remember calling his name, but he didn't respond. When we were leaving the room, Dr. Charles Johnson (a basketball player during his college days) introduced himself, and Mother introduced me. Dr. Johnson said that Dad was in serious but stable condition. Dad had a massive head injury that was putting pressure on his brain, a punctured lung, two broken legs, and numerous bruises. Although he looked bad, he was doing as well as could be expected. After a few days, the swelling from his head injury should go down, releasing the pressure, and no surgery would be needed. Until then, there was nothing else we could do but hope for the best.

"Mother almost shouted, 'I'm doing more than hoping—I'm expecting a full recovery!'

"When Mother and I returned home that evening, I called Valarie and gave her a complete update on Dad and how serious his accident was.

"'Abraham, are you sure I cannot help in some way? I could run some errands while you and your mom are watching your dad.'

"Maurice, I remember how hard it was for me to convince Valarie to stay in school. I told her she probably would do more by praying for Dad than anything else she could think of.

"For the next few days, I relieved Mom when I could convince her to leave Dad's bedside. The swelling from his head injury did go down, but nothing else changed (from what we could see). The days and weeks went by, and there was no physical change in Dad's condition. Dr. Johnson and other employees who knew about Dad were persuaded that the longer he stayed in that sedated condition, the more likely that there would not be a great improvement in his health. Some of them went as far as voicing that opinion. Mom said, 'I don't believe, nor am I going to receive, that conclusion, so if that's all you have to say, please keep it to yourself!'

"It's like I can hear her right now—man, the faith that woman had was amazing.

"After about a month and a half with no significant change in Dad, Mother insisted that I get back to school. Reluctantly, I did as Mom had suggested—knowing that she would let me know of any changes in Dad's condition. The next six months were the hardest I had ever been through. I thought that they would be the hardest I ever would go through. I learned since then that that would not be the case at all. With Dad being seriously ill, graduating from college, entering law school, and Valarie and I spending almost every waking moment together, I did not know if I could handle the heaviness of my load. I knew that the Bible said God would never leave you, but He would be with you every step of the way. As a very young man, I thought, *God I don't know if I am going to make it.* Almost as if on cue God reminded me of the following scripture.

> Come unto me, all ye that labour and are heavy laden,
> and I will give you rest. Take my yoke upon you, and
> Learn of me: for I am meek and lowly in heart:

and ye Shall find rest unto your souls.
For my yoke is easy, and My burden is light (Matthew
11:28–30).

"You know what, Maurice? 'Time heals the brokenhearted' may be
true or not—I'm not sure—but it sure felt like it did. As I said, the first
six months were really tough, but Dad did start to get better. Mom was
by his side all the time, constantly speaking God's word over him and
reminding God, herself, and the devil of the promises God had given her.
Specifically, Mom was thinking and confessing this verse:

Therefore shall a man leave his father and
his mother, and shall cleave unto his wife:
and they shall be one flesh (Genesis 2:24).

"Mom was determined that once she and Dad became one flesh
through marriage, she wasn't going to let the devil or any plot of his break
the bond she had with him. Mom gave Valarie and me updates about
Dad's progress. In the meantime, we both graduated from school with
honors. Dad had been out of danger for some time and was no longer
connected to any machines. In fact, a year and a half had passed since the
accident, and Dad was walking around under his own power—looking
and acting more as he did before the accident. Valarie and I decided to
tell Mom and Dad what they had been expecting for quite some time.

"We took some time off before starting law school. During that
time, we decided to get married. Dad and Mom were so excited; she
could not contain herself, and I thought he was going to start running
(which would have been a miracle). After the test and trial we all had
endured, the thought of a wedding was a blessing. Mom and Valarie
had a ball planning the wedding, and I enjoyed the time I had to spend
with Dad. Valarie's parents were just as excited about the wedding as
mine were. They mentioned to us on more than one occasion that they
thought that we would be getting married because they could tell how
much we loved each other. They did say that because of my dad's ordeal,
they weren't sure when the wedding would take place. With studying
on the back burner for a while, I had fun just relaxing, catching up on
some reading, helping Dad with his rehabilitation, watching the glow on

Valarie's face, and making sure that Mom did not overdo herself. One day, I was sitting in a chair with a book when Dad asked, 'Abraham, what are you reading?'

"'Oh nothing really. I haven't started yet.'"

"'Do you mind waiting a moment? There is something I want to tell you. While I was in the hospital, I want you to know that even though I could not respond, I could tell that your mother was praying for me. I am telling you, Abraham, there is definitely more to life than what we see and hear on earth. I could also hear her confessing.

> But he was wounded for our transgressions, he was bruised for our iniquities: the chastisement of our peace was upon him: and with his stripes, we are healed (Isaiah 53:5).

"'That—and other healing scriptures—seemed to jumpstart my spirit every time she said them. I always knew that God's word was powerful, but this trial took my knowledge and faith in God's word to another level. I know your mother was not talking as loudly as those words were sounding. However, every time she said with authority something that was written in God's word, it sounded like it was coming over a loudspeaker, and my spirit man responded very aggressively. What I mean by that is my physical body could not stay in the condition it was in even if it wanted to. My spirit man had become so strong that my physical body had to respond according to the way my spirit man acted.'"

"Dad said, 'If you don't remember anything else I have said, this you have to get deep down in your spirit man. God's word is not to be taken lightly. Get as much of it as you can operating in your life as soon as you can. I am convinced more now than ever that the body you are looking at is just a housing place for the real person. The real you is inside what we see. If you ever want the person we see to be better than who he is, make the real you (who we do not see) better by spending more time feeding him the word of God. When my spirit man started responding to God's word, that is when my physical body started getting better. God said he confirms his word with signs following.'

"I could tell by looking at Dad and listening to him that he really believed what he was saying—and he was trying to make sure that I understood. Like most everything else in life, some trials you just have to experience before you get the full revelation of what is being revealed to you. As much as I wanted to, I couldn't grasp what Dad was saying to the magnitude that I perhaps should have until much later in life. Oh, I'm almost getting ahead of myself.

"While we were home, Dad was getting better each day. Our marriage ceremony was a joyous occasion and a blessing just having family and friends enjoying it with us. The time was so wonderful. If it was not for the fact that Dad was walking with a cane, you would not have any indication of the struggle that our family had been through. After the honeymoon, which included a cruise, Valarie and I decided that we had better get back to school and resume our studies. Mom and Dad assured us that all was well and everything would be okay. We packed our things and moved into an apartment close to campus."

LAW SCHOOL

"I was excited about entering law school, but I did not have any idea of what the workload would be for a first year law student. In fact, the adjustment was so overwhelming that I took some pre-law classes and waited a year before actually starting. Another reason I chose to wait was so that Valarie and I would be entering law school at the same time. Even though I waited, Valarie and I knew the workload would be quite a bit compared to undergrad. It still was almost too much for me to handle. I thank God for my trust in the Lord and the encouragement of my wife. Maurice, I kid you not, had it not been for Valarie and the Lord, I don't think I would have finished my first year of law school—much less graduated. The many times I seriously considered quitting, I would hear God's words coming up out of my spirit saying, 'I can do all things through Christ which strengtheneth me' (Philippians 4:13). Valarie's adjustment wasn't that hard. As a matter of fact, the times when I was struggling the most, she would tell me that under no circumstances was she going to let me quit. 'We are going to make it," she said.

"Even though the battle was not as intense, those words of encouragement really helped when I needed them most. I learned something that first year in law school that was very influential in not only me graduating, but also in every other task I have pursued in life. As a human being, God gave us the commandment to have dominion over every other thing that he has made (Genesis 1:28). With that revelation and understanding, I was determined that nothing would stop me from achieving every goal I set. Law school was very challenging, but as the months passed, Valarie and I would participate more in group studies, which was very helpful. In fact, it became fun because we understood more and periodically participated in moot court cases on campus. With school being so time consuming, we had to make a conscious effort if we wanted to spend quality time with each other. When there was a holiday or a break from school, we would go home to be with our parents or we would go to a small bed and breakfast to be alone without anyone except us and the Lord.

"The rest of our time in school seemed to go by very fast. I guess that was because of our very busy schedules. With the bulk of our classes ending, we started focusing on internships. During our senior year, I was interning with Krinkle, Plain, and Straight, a law firm in the city, and Valarie interned at the district attorney's office. Immediately after graduation, even though we still worked as interns, we geared most of our time and efforts preparing for the bar exam. Preparing for the bar exam was a stressful time since we both continued to work. Also, understanding how important it was to pass the first time added stress. One thing I thank God for is that both jobs allowed us plenty of time to study. On the day of the exam, we both felt pretty confident. We went in, took the test, and decided to take some time off from work to relax and wait for the results.

"During this time, we realized that God was calling us into ministry. As much as we loved law, we began to understand that God wanted us to be more than lawyers; he wanted us to incorporate what we learned while practicing law into spreading the gospel of Jesus Christ. Maurice, if this sounds confusing to you, imagine how Valarie and I felt when we first figured out that this was what God wanted."

"Excuse me, Abraham, how did you both know that was what God wanted you to do?"

"Well, let me explain. The first thing you need to understand is that humans view marriage differently from how God views it. I can see that puzzled look on your face, so let me continue. When a man and woman get married, it is usually because they love each other, want to raise a family, fulfill God's purpose, and grow old together. That is commendable, but that is not altogether what God has in mind when he puts a man and woman together as husband and wife. God knows that the man cannot fulfill his purpose without that particular woman being there by his side—and likewise the woman cannot fulfill her purpose without that specific man being by her side. When I asked Valarie to marry me, I didn't fully understand that, out of all the women on this planet, she was the one God had put here for me. I did, however, know that I loved her and she was the only woman I wanted to marry and raise a family with. So by marrying each other, we both put ourselves in the position that God wanted us to be in to fulfill our individual purpose and God's divine purpose for our lives.

"Passing the bar exam solidified our employment because we both had been told that permanent positions would be ours for the taking after we passed the bar. I accepted a position with Krinkle, Plain, and Straight— and Valarie accepted a permanent position at the district attorney's office. Once I joined the law firm, I was able to get a lot of experience about various aspects of the law because they did not specialize in any one area. I quickly found myself researching and sometimes even going to court while assisting on criminal, domestic, business, and even cases that had international interest. While I was getting a lot of experience, the job was also demanding, stressful, and time consuming. With as much variety as I had in doing my job, Valarie's was quite the opposite. Most of her experience came while working on criminal cases. Sure, we did our share of work, but we made sure that we took time out for each other. When one of us was overwhelmed with work, we would remind each other that God wanted us to enjoy life—and not get caught up in our jobs. We made ourselves a constant reminder—a scripture we had written in large letters over a mirror in our bedroom.

> For this day is holy unto our Lord:
> Neither be ye sorry; for the joy of the
> Lord is your strength (Nehemiah 8:10).

"We understood that, as long as we kept the joy of the Lord prevalent in our hearts, God would make sure we had the strength to succeed—no matter how stressful things became.

"God revealed the direction that He intended for us to go as far as ministry was concerned. There was a case that involved the law firm where I worked. There were children aged five, eleven, and sixteen whose parents were killed in what appeared to be an accident. Their will stated what should happen to the children in the event that something like this should happen. The suspicion of foul play may cause the specific details in the will not be carried out."

"How could that happen?" I asked. "A will is a legal and binding document, isn't it?"

"Of course it is. Most likely, it would have been administered, but we still had to be aware of the possibility of the unexpected. Maurice, before I continue, I want you to know this was a very traumatic experience for everyone involved. Never have I experienced anything quite that emotional—before or after that case. So, I am going to take my time and try to cover every detail because I want you to get the full impact of how this case affected both me and Valarie. I hope that you can see how it turned us in the direction we went—and have never strayed from in all these years.

"I like to refer to it as the case of my young career. I have seen children in my time and I know that there is no child that is the same, especially where siblings are concerned. These three kids were as opposite as triplets would be alike. You would think that some of the traits or actions they showed would be similar. Robyn, the youngest, was like most six-year-olds. She required and needed affection as much as ever. I could tell that she had been very close and dependent upon her parents, especially her mother. When I first met her months after the accident, even though she understood what had happened, it was evident that it would be quite a while before she would be able to accept what had happened. Tad, the only boy, was quiet and secluded. Getting a simple answer to a simple question was like pulling teeth. I thought that it was okay for a nine-year-old to want to be quiet and keep to himself. It was not out of the ordinary, but that extreme seclusion really bothered me. I spent a lot of time with those children during preparation for the trial. I thought Tad would want to go to the park or a baseball game, but he just was not interested. He would stay in his room unless he was forced out. I was concerned if this developed after his parents death but was told he had always been that way. Mandy, thirteen, was inquisitive and controversial; she always wanted to have her way. 'Why' seemed to be the only word in her vocabulary. The death of their parents affected all the children but I was way off base when I thought that the oldest would be the most understandable. Mark Plain was a friend of the family. The media said that Justin and Tamala Gray's car went over the side while going around a very sharp turn. There was no evidence of the brakes being applied—and it exploded in a ball of fire. Normally, this type of information would not be released to the public, but since it was on a busy road, the police thought it would be better to release the facts to the public to squelch any rumors.

"Matthew Gray, a prominent lawyer, was the father of Justin Gray. He was liked, and respected, and but he chose not to represent his grandchildren in this matter to avoid any signs of impropriety. Even though the police were investigating, Mark Plain let Matthew Gray know that his firm would also investigate and represent his grandchildren in this case.

> I can do all things through Christ which strengthened me (Philippians 4:13).

"Before this case, I thought I knew what Paul meant when God inspired him to write that, but during this case I found that scripture to be manifested in my life very strongly. Everyone at the firm was behind them, but I was not aware how involved I would be.

"Certain events caused me to be closely connected to this case—far more than I anticipated. One day as I was getting ready to leave the office, Mr. Plain asked me to come to his office. When I got there, all three senior partners were in the office. I did not know what to expect, but I knew it was serious because not even one of the partners had ever asked me to a meeting. I was offered a seat, and Mr. Plain began to speak."

"'Abraham, we have been observing you closely since you started working here. From the time that we accepted you as an intern, we noticed how you carry yourself. You make a conscious effort to do whatever is necessary to help everyone in this office—far beyond what anyone would expect. We realize that you haven't been here as long as many of the other employees, but we want to let you know what we are considering if you're interested. We notice that you are intelligent, scored very high on the bar exam, and have a mind for the law that seems to jump off the chart. With that being said, we would like to offer you a full partnership in our firm. Usually, we reserve even thinking about offering this type of partnership to an employee until after they have worked for us for at least ten years. Your presence here has a positive effect on everyone; it is noticeable and addictive. We hired you as an employee, but a person of your caliber and potential could easily become an employee at any of the numerous law firms in the city. What you have is an aura that causes the best to come out of a person—and that is what we do not want to lose (that is what he called it, but I knew it was God's anointing). Well, Abraham, what do you have to say?'

"When Mr. Plain asked me to stop in his office, the last thing I thought was that the senior partners would offer me a full partnership. I was so excited I could hardly contain myself. If you can imagine wanting something very badly and not really knowing how it would become possible—and then it just appeared—no matter how prepared you thought you were, you still would be shocked. I felt as if I had won the lottery. Every fiber in my body wanted to say yes to the offer immediately, but I told them I would get back with a decision if that was okay with them. They insisted that I take time to talk it over with Valarie and get back later with my answer. They told me that they were expecting a favorable answer, but if I decided not to accept the offer, they would understand and proceed with a different course of action. Was this actually happening to me? Was it a dream that I was going to wake up from? Maurice, these thoughts were running through my mind and it was hard for me to grasp, but the word of God spoke to my spirit.

> But as it is written, eye hath not seen, nor ear heard, neither have entered into the heart of man, the things which God hath prepared for them that love him (I Corinthians 2:9).

"I called Valarie immediately and told her not to bother cooking because I wanted to take her out to celebrate. It was hard to concentrate on the drive home but I managed to. As soon as I walked in the door, Valarie rushed into my arms and wanted to know the reason for our celebration. I told her about the partnership offer and she was so thrilled that she yelled at the top of her voice in amazement, *Did you say a full partnership?*

"During dinner, we discussed the pros and cons of the offer, but I was not at peace when I went to bed that night. Maurice, when you really love the Lord and your main desire is to please him in every area of your life, you will not make a decision that will change your life and the people God has connected you with unless you consult him. For a week, I talked with Valarie and my parents, and spent quality, quiet time with the Lord. Maurice, I want you to really listen to what I am about to say. If you are a seasoned Christian—and have a long and strong relationship with the Lord—do not be afraid to make a decision. Not making a choice because you think that you might make the wrong choice is making the wrong choice. It took most of that week to figure that out. I was waiting for God to tell me whether or not to take the position. He was allowing me to make the choice, knowing that I would be happier one way or the other. Even though I did not know the future, God did. The choice I made was the one He wanted for me because I was seeking His direction in the first place.

"Being a full partner was not like lying in a bed of roses, nor was it like being in a bed in hell." It was invaluable to learn about practicing law, how to handle myself while deliberating a closing statement under stressful situations, and hearing clients respond to our representation. I am forever grateful for the opportunity they gave me and for what they saw in me at times when I didn't think I could continue. I just thought that I should say that, Maurice, because I learned in this journey called life that sometimes when we are going through something, we may not fully appreciate what God is teaching us or the person he uses as the teacher.

"Not long after I became a full partner, Mark Plain told me that one of the reasons that they wanted me on board was because they needed someone they had confidence in to take on this case. They were all busy on other high-level cases and did not want to have to worry whether the case would get the attention it needed. They didn't want me to be overwhelmed by my first major case—or have a conflict of interest because of Valarie's position. They offered to move things around so that someone else could take the case. I told them that wouldn't be necessary I would do a very professional job for the firm—and for Gary's grandchildren.

Even though they were young, Robyn, Tad, and Mandy were instrumental in the case. As months passed, I accumulated a lot of information from revisiting the crash site numerous times, evaluating lab reports, and pondering what could have caused this crash. I built what

I thought was a strong case. Friends of the children's parents, relatives, and even acquaintances weren't able to give me any reason or indication why Justin or Tamala would take their own lives. Actually, all evidence agreed with the police report that this was an accidental death."

"Excuse me, Abraham. If everyone—the police department, the district attorney's office, and your firm—agreed that this was an accidental death, why the investigation?"

"Well, even though they were a wealthy family, they still had insurance coverage. Most insurance companies want a very detailed investigation before any money is paid out. Although Valarie was working for the district attorney's office and this wasn't a criminal case, I would discuss specific parts of the case with her. Perhaps she could shed some light on why I couldn't sign off on the case as an accidental death. There was no reason for this car to veer off the road and, knowing this, no insurance company would pay the claim. In the insurance company's view, if this was an accidental death as everyone claimed, then there had to be physical proof of the cause. That was bothering me and is why, in my spirit, I could not let it go. Valarie said that if I didn't have any hard evidence to prove otherwise, then circumstantial evidence would have to do. I couldn't prolong the ending. I knew that my partners and Matthew Gray wanted the case to end to get some closure for his grandchildren and the rest of the family.

"I was sure that the insurance company wanted this case finalized more than anyone else because, without hard physical evidence proving that this was an accidental death, they could file that the policy couldn't be paid based on circumstantial evidence. Even though that may have been the legal ramification, I just couldn't stop—not right then—I was missing something. Valarie said that she was in my corner for as long as it took. She trusted that the Holy Spirit would direct me all the way to the end. A conclusion, finalization, or an end—however anyone tried to spin this case—not everyone wanted a lengthy procedure. My heart felt that it was not complete. My partners wanted to know the status of the case and a timetable for a trial—if it came to that.

"As we gathered in the conference room, I explained that it would be pretty difficult to have a trial if first proof that a crime had been committed wasn't established—and second there wasn't a suspect to bring to trial.

I knew that cases are concluded based on facts, but I was not convinced that we had everything and I refused to stop researching."

"'Abraham,' Mark interjected, 'you cannot let your heart allow your decision to become clouded. Remember the facts. Justin and Tamala were well liked and did not have any known enemies. They were prominent; very, very wealthy; involved in the community; their family is respected and known all over the country; there was no foul play at the scene; and their children have a host of family and friends who would be more than happy to take them in.'

"'Mark, I understand the facts, but you have all forgotten what no one seems to want to mention—what the person with custody of the children would receive out of the will.'"

"I continued, 'The money that would be granted to the custodian of the children could perhaps be the motive for someone to kill them— if they didn't know that Justin and Tamala wanted his father to be the executor of the will and would determine what amount would be designated to the custodian of the children. Additionally, the Grays put in their will that the children's godparents and their best friends would be the custodians. Everyone who knew Justin and Tamala knew that their closest friends were Reginald and Ingrid Myles.

"'Ingrid is an old college roommate of Tamala. The Myles are also very wealthy. The insurance company lawyers and the police investigation verified that they were out of the country at the time of the accident—and had been for quite a while on business. The inheritance of $100 million per child could definitely be a motive, but that is ruled out because their will stated that no one under any circumstance could get their hands on it. This money was going into an interest-bearing account that would be released to each child upon reaching adulthood.'"

"As we were about to end the meeting, I said, 'Gentlemen, I have a suggestion. Give me three days and I guarantee I'll have a conclusion to this case.'

"John asked, 'How are you going to do in three days what you have not been able to do all this time?'

"'Don't worry. If I haven't found the answer I'm looking for then in three days, I'll turn it over to the district attorney's office as an accidental death because I will have peace in my spirit knowing that everything that needed to be done was done indeed.'

"Cautiously, the partners agreed and said they would be looking forward to hearing from me. After leaving the office and arriving home, I told Valarie that I needed to go on a sabbatical. There was something I wanted to know that only God could answer. I didn't want to do it without her approval because she was my wife and God's daughter.

"'Honey, you know whenever you need to get alone with the Lord, I don't mind at all. I know it is very important and serious. I also understand that some questions require time alone with the Lord to get the correct answer. So, go ahead, Abraham—take as much time as you need. I'll be praying for your strength and revelation during that time.'

"Maurice, I learned early in life that some things require a sacrifice on my part in order to get a desired result. Going on a sabbatical gave me the opportunity to clear everything out of my mind so that I could hear clearly from the Lord. Sometimes there may be so much going on in your life that even though you may be doing the right thing—researching, studying, asking the right questions, or getting good advice—it still may not give you the peace you need. Getting alone with the Lord and putting yourself in a position where you can hear Him clearly is the only way you will ever be able to solve some of life's toughest problems.

> Be careful for nothing; but in every thing
> By prayer and supplication with thanksgiving
> Let your requests be made known unto God.
> And the peace of God, which passeth all
> Understanding, shall keep your hearts and
> minds through Christ Jesus (Philippians 4:6–7).

"I went on this sabbatical to find out from the Lord why I wasn't getting peace in my spirit with the results I was getting in this case. During those three days, God told me that everyone was correct. There wasn't any foul play. The death of Justin and Tamala Gray was an accident and it was not avoidable.

"The Lord said to my spirit, 'While on the outside, Justin and Tamala appeared to be the perfect couple, they were lacking a very important part in their life. They had a wonderful marriage, loving children, and an impeccable reputation, but they didn't have total trust in Me for everything. Those loving children—so everyone thought—are what killed them. Justin and Tamala were constantly worrying over those children. Yes, the children were very different from each other—that's the way I made them and because they were acting out their different personalities in ways their parents didn't understand, instead of trusting Me and seeking My direction for their lives, Justin and Tamala Gray tried to handle it themselves. Abraham, as a result of their actions, the pressure of trying to orchestrate every part of those children's lives—especially as they got older—became too much of a burden even though they didn't recognize it as being that.'

"'As they were driving home, a vessel burst in Justin's brain. It caused him to black out and drive off the road. Even though the coroner did an autopsy, because his brain was burned beyond recognition, the DNA results would not have this information. So be at peace, my son, and remember what you have learned in the past. I am always here waiting for you to stop your busy schedule and seek My input in your life.'

"I met with John, Mark, and Luke not long after completing my sabbatical and explained what happened. I said, 'Let's see if the coroner can find what type of effect a ruptured vessel would have on any other part of the remains. With this added information and proof, we can close this case, and all parties with a vested interest—especially the insurance company—can be assured that no foul play was involved in their deaths.' The partners were amazed by how I knew exactly what had happened.

"Noticing their expressions, I explained that I had asked God for the answer. I said, 'I have learned over the years—because of my relationship with the Lord—if I ask him something specifically and wait, He will answer. This is the type of relationship He wants with not only me—but with all who seek him.'

"The partners thanked me and John asked, 'Abraham, if that is all it took for you to get the answer, why didn't you do it sooner?' I told him even seasoned Christians sometimes forget to seek God first.

"Years after I had that case and numerous others under my belt, an urging in my spirit was becoming stronger. I said, 'Honey, our careers are going well and God is blessing us mightily, but for some reason I'm getting an impression in my spirit that there is something else God wants us to do.'

"Valarie also felt a similar call, but we couldn't decide if we were called to ministry or raising a family. We decided to pray so that we would know exactly what God wanted us to do. With that being said, Maurice, I suggest we stop until next time. After all, Rome wasn't built in a day."

FAMILY TIME

"Hello, Abraham. I know th-th-this is the third interview, but I can hardly wait. I anticipate it-it-it will be as exciting as the previous meetings."

"Good afternoon, Maurice. I'm glad you are enjoying these interviews, but excitement isn't exactly what I was aiming for. I must admit that my life wasn't—and isn't—boring by any stretch of the imagination. If you are ready, let's get started. For most of the following year, Valarie and I focused on our careers, praying at length about raising a family and pursuing the ministry God wanted us to do. It was a major decision—and my biggest concern was missing God's perfect will because of our own will.

"The family question was answered rather easily. While we were seeking God's direction on when—or even if—we should start raising a family, Valarie started having pregnancy symptoms. Amazingly, now that I think about it, we were not doing anything to keep from having a child then or ever since we got married. Therefore, starting a family for us was in God's control all the time.

"We didn't start out with that philosophy. Also, we didn't decide that intentionally we weren't going to use any type of birth control—if Valarie got pregnant, it would be God's will. What happened, as far-fetched as it may sound, was that two educated adults never even thought that we might have a child before we were ready. As much as I would like to say that we used our faith and trusted that God would keep her from getting pregnant before we were ready—without us using any kind of precautions—that wasn't the case. In fact, that would have been foolish thinking on both of our parts. The only conclusion we were able to come up with was that there must have been something medically keeping her from becoming pregnant. Since she wasn't trying to become pregnant, we never considered that perhaps she couldn't. With the doctor's confirmation that Valarie was truly pregnant, we were satisfied that it was God telling us to start a family.

"Even though we were seeking God's will and timing to raise a family, in spite of our ignorance, it happened anyway. We wanted to start our family when God said it was time, but what we actually did had absolutely no bearing on God's decision. Maurice, do you remember when I told you the story of my dad's car breaking down?"

"Yes," I said. "I asked how you learned to know what God wanted you to do and when."

"I told you that I would tell you at a later date. Since timing with God is very important, we try to adjust our schedule to His timing when we do not have a clue what it is. The reason we don't know God's timing is because, with God, there is no such thing as time in the way we know it. We look at time in seconds, minutes, hours, days, weeks, months, and years, but God looks at time from the aspect of beginning and ending. When we try to do something in God's timing, we cannot actually calculate what God's time is because God already knows the outcome of all that is to be done.

"Simply put, if you want to do something and you want it to be done in God's perfect will and timing, just do it. If it is not God's will or timing, you will not be able to accomplish any task without considerable difficulty. Since the enemy would not want you to do it in the first place and without God's approval, you would not have His protection and provision. On the other hand, if it is His perfect will and timing, He will provide you with protection and provision. Everything we receive from God is a gift.

> Every good gift and every perfect gift is from above,
> And cometh down from the Father of lights,
> With Whom is no variableness, neither shadow of
> turning (James 1:17).

"That scripture refers to ideas, dreams, visions, and talents. If God did not want you to do a thing, you never would have come up with the idea in the first place. Nobody is that smart. That is something I learned a long time ago.

"We both were overjoyed at the confirmation of Valarie's pregnancy. During the first months, everything was normal. The closer we got to the delivery date, the more time Valarie spent with my parents. The pregnancy was going as expected without complications, but Valarie felt more comfortable being closer to Mother because of their relationship and she was experienced in that area.

"Micah was a textbook baby. His early years went almost exactly the way the experts said they would. He was rambunctious, energetic, and curious. He was a handful, but we enjoyed that time very much. He grew into a very intelligent young man. As you know, he is the CEO of Caldwell Ministries. Maurice, one of the greatest things I am proud of is how Micah and his wife, Elizabeth, have continued with the ministry.

"As much joy as it was raising Micah, Joy was a different story altogether. Until her early adolescent years, saying raising her was a challenge would be an understatement. If I didn't know any better, I would have said that she was accident-prone, but I know that was just a lie from the pit of hell. Valarie and I knew she was a blessing from God."

The blessing of the Lord, it maketh rich,
And he addeth no sorrow with it (Proverbs 10:22).

"Even though we knew and believed that God is faithful to His Word, our faith was tried where Joy was concerned. When she was six, Joy seemed to be getting more bumps, bruises, and scrapes than other children her age—and she definitely had more than Micah did when he was that age. Those incidents seem minor in comparison to the battle we had when she started having headaches at thirteen. We couldn't figure out what the problem was. She said that her head didn't hurt all the time—only when she concentrated, like for a test. We took her to the doctor after praying and he gave her a prescription. The headaches lessened, but didn't stop. Finally, we decided to take her to a specialist.

"With all of this going on, Maurice, can you imagine what the devil was speaking to my mind? For example, the devil would say, 'Look at how much God loves you, Faith Child, and this is happening to your daughter.' The devil also spoke a constant flow of negativity about how my child was going to die from some type of brain tumor. Valarie and I were praying and believing God, but I couldn't let her know what was coming to my mind. She tried her best not to let me know how the devil was attacking her mind also, but I knew that if he was attacking me, then she was being attacked as well. We encouraged each other with scriptures and made a conscious effort not to let Joy get any inclination of us wavering in our faith. This was one battle I knew—according to God's word—that I already had victory over. To be honest with you, I am not sure that I really believed it.

"I am glad my father was still around during that time. I went to him when fighting that unbearable battle and I let him know exactly what was going on in my mind. He told me to remember what he said about the literal power of God's word and that I have the Spirit of the almighty God on the inside and the word of the Lord Jesus at my access. He told me to use what was available—and find a scripture that is tailor-made for my situation. I should meditate on it until it became larger than anything else in my mind. Later, Valarie and I should go in the power and authority that God has given and let the devil know that I know who I am. We should command him to take his hands off our baby.

"I told Valarie about our discussion and we decided whose report we were going to believe. We prayed, repented for doubting, and asked for forgiveness. As the Holy Spirit led us, He directed us to the following scripture:

> Again I say unto you, that if two of
> You shall agree on earth as touching
> Anything that they shall ask, it shall be
> Done for them of my Father which is
> in heaven (Matthew 18:19).

"We confessed and thanked God for confirmation of His word. Joy was healed and made whole. I meditated for three days on Matthew 18:19. When that time was up, I took Valarie's hand and we approached the devil in the power and authority of Jesus Christ. I understood the full revelation of what my father had told me about the power in God's word. From that moment on, I have never felt like I was not victorious in a battle. Oh, there have been opportunities, but when you get the full revelation of the power of God's word, you will stand. Valarie and I told the devil to take his hands off Joy's health—and all other areas of her life—and never come back. We told him that we were not asking or begging—we were commanding him in the mighty name of Jesus Christ.

"While we were continuing to develop our faith, we continued to take Joy to the specialist—but it didn't look like the situation was changing. One day while we were watching television, Joy came in the room from doing her homework wearing her brother's glasses. We asked why and she said that she had asked Micah if she could try them on to see what they felt like. Her head didn't hurt like it usually did when she finished studying. We wondered if it was possible that the answer could be that simple.

"Maurice, I know you are thinking that someone should have thought about glasses much earlier. Maybe that's true, but when the attacks started—with the severity of each one and the negative information the devil was sending—I guess we were so close to the situation that we overlooked what was right in front of us all the time. As far as the professionals thinking of the possibility of glasses, I believe that God was using that opportunity to teach us how to use His Word and our faith in Christ to get a desired result.

"Yes, God is awesome! Whenever we allow the peace of God to cover us and settle our minds, we put ourselves in a position to hear when He speaks and recognize His deliverance—no matter how he chooses to do it. The next day, we took Joy to the doctor and explained to him what had happened. He immediately made an appointment with an eye specialist. After an extensive examination, the specialist was able to tell us the problem.

"When Joy would read or concentrate heavily, she was straining her optic nerve and putting pressure on an area of her brain that was causing the headaches. When she put on her brother's glasses—because of how long she had them on—they kept her from straining her optic nerve and avoiding the pressure on her brain that was causing the headaches. The specialist recommended reading glasses to strengthen her eyes. After a while, she would not need glasses and the headaches would disappear. Joy wore glasses for a year—and her headaches stopped completely within eight months. From then on, Joy hasn't had a headache or any headache symptoms."

MINISTRY

"After Valarie and I got married and started working full time, we joined a local church where we were members for more than a decade. The church wasn't large in comparison with the size of the more established churches in the area. There were about fifty members when we started going. The services were lively and the members were friendly. We made a commitment to that ministry because the pastor's messages were inspirational and challenging. During that time, we worshipped and faithfully worked in our church doing whatever we felt God led us to do. Valarie and I taught Sunday school—and I was called by God to preach the Gospel of our Lord Jesus Christ.

I asked, "Abraham, how did you know that God called you to be a preacher?"

"That is a very good question, Maurice. Let me explain. First, preaching is telling the good news of Jesus Christ, which is every child of God's responsibility. But being called to be a preacher or pastor is something God ordains for an individual to do well before that person is born."

> Before I formed thee in the belly I knew thee:
> And Before thou camest forth out of the womb
> I sanctified thee, and ordained thee a prophet unto
> the nations (Jeremiah 1:5).

"If God called Jeremiah to be a prophet before he was born, He also called me to do the work I am doing before I was born. I later understood that whether I recognized the calling or not, it was still there. Doing what God ordained for me to do does not change His purpose for my life. The call is always there. If I had not acknowledged and obeyed it, when I stand before Jesus Christ, I would still be judged according to that call.

> For we must all appear before the judgement seat of Christ; that everyone may receive the things done in His body according to that he hath done whether it be Good or bad (II Corinthians 5:10).

"Since I recognized the call to walk in the pastoral office, my next greatest concern was being in God's timing.

"One of the most important things you will ever learn is not only to be in God's perfect will, but also His timing. You may be moving in God's perfect will—doing exactly what He says to do—but if you miss His timing, you will miss what He has for you at that time because you will be out of place. That creates a couple more questions. How do I know when it is God's timing and what do I do until that time comes? I will answer the last part first. What do I do until that time comes? Continue doing what you are doing and do not try to make any changes. As you continue doing the last thing God has instructed you to do and stay before Him in prayer and quiet time, He will let you know when it is time to change course or do something different. Next, how will I know when it is God's timing? When the time comes for you to move on what you know God told you to do, pieces will start to fall in place. Those things that you have been waiting to do—or it may seem like that is all you can focus on or think about—the opportunity to pursue them will present itself. It will seem miraculous how events will fall into place. Trust me. When that time comes, you will know.

"I briefly mentioned the ministry, but I never went into full detail. Around the time that Valarie and I were involved in the Justin and Tamala Gray case, God again stirred up ministry in my spirit. The first time was when Valarie and I were still in college. The second time was while I was at Krinkle, Plain, and Straight. The third time was when we started our family. Maurice, if you noticed, God let me know that ministry was the direction He wanted me to go three times. Even though that was God's will for my life and I knew it, He still did not force me to go that way. He allowed me to pursue my dreams until I realized that the fulfillment I was looking for wasn't in law. Although I didn't jump right into ministry immediately, I never forgot that the call was there.

"Now, this is surprising about the ministry that God ordained for us. As much as we thought and tried to turn this ministry God had entrusted in our hands into what we wanted or what we thought God wanted it to be, God would not let us do that. Like most ministries, we thought that God wanted us to establish a church locally, help those in the local community as our church grew, and do some additional work in the area of outreach. Boy, we sure were surprised when God caused our ministry to blossom in ways we never even imagined. The way this ministry turned out and the success we have had all these years, in all my wildest dreams I could not have came up with a design or plan that would have produced these kinds of results. So I knew it had to be God.

"When we started, I knew that God wanted this ministry to be debt free from the onset. I did not have any idea where the money was coming from to start this ministry part-time much less full-time—and that is what God was revealing in my spirit. Valarie and I did have some money saved. After all, we were both lawyers and practicing law is an economically sound career. Valarie and I were more than willing to use our money in the ministry if God told us to, but it is His ministry. I believe that God is more than able to finance His ministry without depending on our finances. That He did—and how He did it—is still amazing to me. God let me know from the beginning that this would be a seed-sowing ministry.

"Yes, our ministry would be like others in that we would have a church building, Sunday and weekly services, and minister the full uncompromised Gospel of Jesus Christ. We would expand in some areas of outreach. But in one area, perhaps more than any other ministry, we would be a channel that God would use to be a financial blessing to the body of Christ and mankind as a whole. Now, this is what was so amazing to me. The church we were affiliated with for some time was no longer the place where God wanted us to continue to worship. After much prayer—and our pastor's blessing—we were confident that Jesus wanted us to leave, but we didn't know where He wanted us to go.

"Even though we didn't have a particular church or church home we were committed to, we continued paying our tithe—it is still God's money. Instead of paying our tithe to God through a church, we opened a bank account that we kept strictly for that purpose. I was surprised by how much accumulated in that account so quickly. No matter how large that account grew, if God didn't instruct us on where to sow that money, we continued to put our tithe in it and nothing was taken out of it. Even though I knew the Lord wanted us to start the ministry like I know my own name, I still didn't know exactly when He wanted me to go full-steam ahead.

"One day a local businessman by the name of Billy Griffin called me and said that God told him I was in need of a building. He had an old building that we could have. This was one of those times when you ask God for provisions and—even though you believe he is going to supply the need—you are still shocked when it happens. Exactly two years after we started putting God's money in a separate account, Mr. Griffin contacted me. Billy gave us the building with no strings attached, but Jesus told us that his business was the first we were to sow into. At the time, I thought it was a substantial seed. Sowing twenty-five thousand dollars at one time into one place was the largest seed we had ever given. Yes, it was God's money, but I would be lying if I told you that I was not apprehensive about giving such a large amount.

"The building was large enough to seat about one hundred adults in the main area. It had two additional rooms and male and female bathrooms. We modified it a little to make a pulpit, and used one of the extra rooms for an office and the other for classes.

"I don't know about other ministries that start from just a pastor and his family but I wasn't sure how this ministry was going to grow. I thought I should go back to our church and let the pastor help—even though I knew in my spirit that it wasn't what God wanted. I also thought perhaps I should go around and hand out flyers announcing our grand opening, but I didn't get peace in my spirit to go in that direction either. I told Valarie that we were to let those close to us—family members, neighbors, and co-workers—know that we were starting Caldwell Ministries, Incorporated. As God directed, we would let them know when our first services would begin. The attendance at the first service was ten adults and children in addition to Valarie, Micah, Joy, and me. I was delighted and excited with that turnout.

"No one wants to be a failure. As much as I knew in my heart and spirit that God wanted me to start this ministry, I was more confident when more than my family was at that first service. I would have continued if we were the only people there, but it sure helped strengthen my faith to know that I was truly walking the faith walk—and not just talking the faith talk—when others showed up.

"That first service was a surprise, but that was small in comparison to the first year. Caldwell Ministries grew to over two hundred and fifty adults in that first year. With the growth of the ministry and the demands on my time, I tried working as a part-time partner with the law firm, but eventually had to quit and went into ministry full-time. A year later, Valarie quit working for the district attorney's office and worked full-time in the ministry.

"I have learned that as long as I clearly understand the instructions I receive from the Lord and do as He says, everything—and I do mean everything—will turn out fine. God said this ministry would primarily be a channel of financial blessings for the body of Christ and mankind as a whole. Well, what God meant was *the whole body of Christ*—not just the part in our local community. I don't think I fully understood the full revelation of what God was telling me until perhaps the fourth or fifth year. It was the first time that this kind of ministry was done, to the best of my knowledge. The building was paid for and we still had God's tithe in that separate account. The only bills we had were operating expenses and we were still sowing seed into other ministries."

> Will a man rob God? Yet ye have robbed me. But ye say, Wherein have we robbed thee in tithes and offerings you are cursed with a curse: for ye have robbed me, even this whole nation. Bring ye all the tithes into the storehouse, that there may be meat in mine house, and prove me now herewith saith the Lord of hosts, if I will not open you the windows of heaven and pour you out a blessing that there shall not be room enough to receive it. And I will rebuke the devourer for your sakes (Malachi 3:8–11).

"In this particular passage, God let us know that not paying tithe would be robbing Him. In contrast, as we obey Him by paying tithe,

He would give unlimited financial blessings. Even though that is what God promised in scripture, it is not what he told me specifically. God told me that even though He said a tithe in Malachi (which is 10 percent of any increase I receive), He wanted 90 percent of what comes into this ministry to go out as a seed offering and 10 percent to be used for operating expenses. Now you're probably thinking *just* 10 percent for operating expenses. Why, that's impossible. How can a business— especially a non-profit ministry—operate on just 10 percent of what comes in? If you think about it, no business can—but with God in the business, nothing is impossible.

"Before that first service, we transferred the tithing money into an account for Caldwell Ministries, Incorporated. Starting with that first service—and even now—90 percent of all monies that come into Caldwell Ministries is sown into other ministries and 10 percent is used for Caldwell Ministries. We had this written into the bylaws of the official documents when the ministry was established. Every person who became a member or worked at Caldwell Ministries understood this.

"Although Caldwell Ministries operates for the most part like any other ministry, in this area it is very different—and because it is what God told me to do, we were able to do just that. Maurice, I know this might be redundant but I have to make it clear, no matter what type of ministry and/or business you have, there is no logical way (according to man, that is) it will survive—especially in the early stages—on only 10 percent of the income that's received. If God did not orchestrate the direction of this ministry, I am convinced that it definitely would have failed. At the end of the first year, we looked at how God had caused increases in our membership, operating budget, and sowing account. We were totally in awe. God is awesome!

"Most times you will not be able to see God's movement in your daily life, but when you look back, you will be able to see how God's influence affected your outcome. As the years passed, I have noticed that whenever we were about to be confronted with something out of the ordinary, God would have us sow a substantial seed. You might say, 'Well, it is God's money anyway.' While that is true, God still holds us accountable as stewards, so we couldn't just throw the money away. What God did in the early years of the ministry would eventually seem small, but at the time, it was very large. God used the ministry as a channel to bless the body of Christ financially. That is the best way I can describe how God caused trillions of dollars to flow through this ministry. There are so many ministries that God has allowed Caldwell Ministries to be a blessing to. I am not at liberty to mention the names and, unless God told me, I wouldn't do it anyway. Anyone's faith can be strengthened while continuing to do what Jesus tells him or her to do. After five years the membership had grown to more than 1550 of the most faithful and generous members you could ask for. As a result of the increase in our membership and finances, God blessed us to sell that original building and build a new facility.

"That building is still located on same the property as our main sanctuary. When we first purchased that land, God told us that He would give us favor to buy over one hundred of the surrounding acres. At the time, we didn't have the money to purchase all the land, but we were guaranteed that we would always have the option to purchase before anyone else. As we continued to obey God, we have been able to purchase all the land He promised us. Even though our ministry was sowing on a regular basis into other ministries, I remember the first time that God told us to bless a particular ministry that was struggling.

"At a conference, we saw a pastor from a third world country ministering at a service. Since Valarie and I knew Caldwell Ministries was a seed-sowing ministry, we asked God before we left for direction as to what and how we should sow while at the conference. The amount came first while we were on the plane. Valarie and I were relaxing when an elderly woman approached us. She said, 'I know you don't know me, but God told me to tell you $250,000. I don't have any idea what that means, but I'm just doing what God told me to do.' We knew exactly what it meant. She didn't ask or pressure us for an explanation and neither did we volunteer one. We knew what that meant because we were expecting an answer from the Lord pertaining what to sow at the conference—and that was all we had left in Caldwell Ministries' account.

"If God ever requires you to give all you have—I don't care about the size or the amount—the enemy will immediately unleash an astronomical number of reasons as to why you can't or shouldn't do it. To avoid this temptation, the first chance we got, we called home and told our financial administrator to go to the bank, get a cashier's check for the full amount, and mail it to us as fast as possible.

"I learned that, when anyone gets confirmation from God on what to do, they should do it as soon as possible. It doesn't matter if it is giving something, saying something, going somewhere, or anything else God tells them to do, if they procrastinate about doing that very thing, they will not do it. I understand that there may be a timing issue, but if you really want to do something, you will. Additionally, you don't ever want to give place to the devil.

"Satan will use every trick he can to keep you from doing anything that causes advancement to the Kingdom of God. Satan knows that if anyone is willing to do whatever it takes to be an instrument for God, he or she cannot be stopped. He tries to stop him or her before or while they are in the process of making that decision. Maurice, you need to understand that $250,000 is a very large—I do mean large—amount of money. Right now, it does not seem nearly as much as it did then because we have grown. But—trust me—even though it was God's money, we were still entrusted to do what is right.

"Maurice, there were ministry needs of the church that we could have pursued with that money—especially when it was all we had. This particular conference lasted seven days and we knew that God wanted the money to go to a specific individual during that time. Although there were numerous opportunities for us to give—and we did—that still did not stop us from sowing seed into the ministry God told us to. There was no doubt in my mind or spirit that we did what God said. I was more confident than ever that God was going to do what he promised.

"Hold onto your seat because what I am going to tell you is the absolute truth. Even though I don't have to, let me know and I will show you proof. Exactly two weeks after returning from the conference, we received a certified check in the mail from a company called Doing God's Will, Incorporated for $550,000. I had never heard of that company and was curious about the legitimacy of the check. I researched and found it to be a legal company. During a conversation with someone there, I found out that check was sent to us because the owner of the company gave the order. His name was never made known to me so I accepted the check on behalf of Caldwell Ministries and we praised God for his faithfulness.

"A week later, we received another check for $800,000 from the uncle of Lottie Bingham, a member of our church. Fuad James was a businessman who received a very large bonus on a stock investment. He didn't have any children of his own so he wanted to do something—not only for her, but also her church.

"This was one of the most amazing things I experienced in the financial area of Caldwell Ministries. A month after receiving the check from Fuad James, I received another check for over $1 million. One day, a man whom I'll call Roger—I'm not sure that's his real name—came to me and told me while he was in prayer earlier that week the Lord Jesus told him to give me the money. The money wasn't a problem because he had more than he could ever spend during his lifetime. What alarmed him was how God described me to him. God told him to go to the law firm and ask them about the person that they were most impressed by and that was who he was to give this money to. Roger and I spent the rest of the afternoon in my office because he wanted to know what about me had impressed them and why God wanted him to give me that much money. I told him briefly about myself. I wanted him to meet Valarie, but he couldn't because God wanted him to be as unknown as possible. He told me this wasn't the first time he had given a large sum of money under God's direction—and it probably would not be the last. As long as he lived, he said that he would never forget our talk. In a little more than two months, we were blessed with more than $2 million.

"I am humble and in awe at what God has done—and is still doing—for Caldwell Ministries and my family. From the time we emptied our account to the time we received that first check, Caldwell Ministries has never been without.

"As I reflect, I can see how the hand of God has been instrumental in the way my life has developed. God chose to use me as a blessing and a tool to touch many lives—and I am truly grateful. In no way am I better or special than anyone else. What I did try to do—and stayed conscious of—is making myself available for God's use. I have learned over the years that I am not a superman. I may not be able to complete everything I try—and I may make mistakes while trying—but God is full of mercy and His grace is more than sufficient. Don't beat yourself up. Remember that life is a journey and—like all journeys—preparation before and adjustments during the trip must be made if you expect to get to your final destination."

For which of you intending to build a tower, sitteth

not down first and counteth the cost, whether he have sufficient to finish it (Luke 14:28).

"Maurice, God always has blessed me immensely. Micah and Joy are doing wonderfully. They have families of their own and are working diligently for Caldwell Ministries. I'm pretty sure that you are aware of that since the ministry is in the news as much as it is. Micah Caldwell and Joy Caldwell-Young are practically household names. I am so glad that Valarie and I had some success with the ministry and could leave it as a blessing to our next generation. I am pleased that Micah and Joy are doing a marvelous job without us—and I am so glad that they are continuing to learn to trust the Lord for themselves."

The Philanthropist

―――――――――――

"Well, Maurice, this is the final interview. I have enjoyed every moment we have spent together. I trust it has not been a disappointment to you."

"No, Abraham. You will never know how much of a blessing this has been to me. I knew that there was something special about your life because of how long you have lived—but I didn't have any idea how special."

"Let me remind you that my life is not all that special. What is special is my relationship with Jesus. He is the one—and only one—who makes the rest of my life seems special. You know what else? This special relationship is more than available to anyone who wants it. "As Caldwell Ministries grew over the years, Valarie and I gradually stepped out of the limelight. Under the direction of the Lord, we let Micah and Joy take it to the next phase that God wanted for them. Although we were not in the public eye nearly as much as before, we were helping behind the scenes sometimes and were always there for them. So, what did we do?

"For the past thirty years, we have been so blessed—especially financially—that God has kept his promise. He has literally been using us as a channel to be a financial blessing to the body of Christ and mankind as a whole. With the retirement from our law careers and wise investments from our personal finances, we have been able to bless other individuals, charities, and other ministries with over ten billion dollars between Caldwell Ministries and our personal income. There are so many ministries, causes, and people in need. The more we became able to help in those areas, the more we became aware of how God wanted to use us as a blessing.

"Over twenty years ago, I had a dream that I was driving a car—not necessarily leaving or going anywhere particular—just driving. I eventually ended up driving on a four-lane highway that was spiraling upward. Every time one lane was about to end, another one would start. I would change to the new lane and keep going. I never did get to the end before I woke up. I never told anyone about that dream, but I did notice that our personal financial situation changed dramatically.

"When God gets ready to release something of major proportion in your hands, He requires a great sacrifice. A sacrifice is not something you cannot do. It is something you can do but the hard part is deciding whether you are willing to do it. For years, there was something I wanted to do that was based on something that happened in my life, but the opportunity to make it happen never presented itself. Even though this event happened before I met Valarie, I told her about it because periodically God would bring it to my memory.

"Not long after the driving dream, I saw someone whom I had not seen in over thirty years ministering on television. When I saw him, I was stunned. I called to Valarie and she ran in. I said, 'That's him. That's the guy I've been talking about. His parents helped me out a long time ago.' We sat down and watched the entire show. Afterward, there was an appeal made and—even though I had not seen this person in over thirty years—I knew that it was time to fulfill my desire to be a blessing to him that I had not been able to do before. Whether to answer the appeal and be a blessing to him and his ministry wasn't the question—just how much of a blessing God wanted us to be was the question. I knew what I wanted to give—based only on my feelings—but I didn't say anything to Valarie. We just prayed.

"After praying and waiting for instructions from the Lord, I told Valarie that I was told $5.5 million and she informed me that God confirmed the same amount in her spirit. It would be—by far—the most we had given at one time to any single entity. We gave what God said, and as far as I know, the only people who know what we gave are me, Valarie, this particular gentleman, and God. That's the way God wanted it—so that's what we did. Even though we have only spoken a few times since then, both he and his ministry have been—and still are—a blessing to millions of people.

"When Valarie and I semi-retired from Caldwell Ministries, we still wanted to do more in other areas—not necessarily connected with the ministry—to help others. That desire is a big part of the motivation behind the hospitals we built. You know what, Maurice? It is hard to do any project of a large magnitude without your name and the event becoming well known. The hospitals we built in Florida, California, and New York are examples of what I mean. We never thought building those hospitals would bring as much attention to us as they did. We purposely did as much as we could to make sure our names would remain behind the scenes.

"The Susan Caldwell Hospital of Florida—our first one—was a vision given to Valarie. She and Mother had become so close over the years that, when Mom went home to be with the Lord, Valarie took it very hard—much harder than I did—even though her death was expected."

> We are confident, I say, and willing rather to be absent from the body, and to be present with the Lord (II Corinthians 5:8).

"We are emotional humans—and their strong bond was broken. No matter how much Valarie tried to prepare herself for when Mother left, it still wasn't easy. Mom did not die from a tragic accident or illness of any type. She just, for the lack of a better term, wore out. She was ready—and Valarie agreed, but she found it to be more difficult than she expected.

"Valarie wanted to do something for Mom. She didn't want it to be something that would only be remembered on her birthday or the anniversary of her death—she wanted it to be something that would be remembered every day and used by countless people. God has blessed us so that money is no object, but we are still held accountable for what we do with it. I told Valarie to pray and ask God for direction. He impressed in her spirit to build a hospital. I figured that she wanted to add a wing onto the local hospital in Mom's honor—a wonderful idea. I was wrong—she told me that God wanted us to build a hospital that will never charge anyone who comes in—from the time they get there until they leave. The hospital would be continually funded by us and anyone else God chooses. Its mission would be to minister to the physical and spiritual man. No one would ever be turned away—and everyone would be given an opportunity to accept the gift of salvation given by Jesus Christ.

"Maurice, you need to understand how serious Valarie was about the spiritual aspect of this hospital. This hospital would function like any other hospital in the country besides the strong spiritual influence it would have on anyone affiliated with it—doctors, lawyers, patients, administrative staff, and anyone else attached to the hospital in any way. I know that having a hospital run by people who are born again and committed to do things God's way sounds like a far-fetched idea, but we were determined that the hospital would be built and run how God had told us. Nothing and nobody would stop us.

"This was no easy task by any stretch of the imagination. One thing I will admit is that after the Susan Caldwell Hospital was up and running, the others were easier to get going. The other building projects we were involved in either directly or indirectly—we were lawyers, after all—gave us some experience in knowing what to expect as far as bureaucracy. All of that was well and good, but the fight we encountered because of the spiritual implications was exactly that. What we wanted to do was something that had never been done in the health care industry. We wanted the business obligated by law to pay taxes; adhere to all the laws that applied to this type of business; as well as administer to the health care of anyone and everyone that came in. We also wanted to have included in our bylaws that anyone—employee or patient—would agree to the Gospel of Jesus Christ being shared as well as the administration of medical services.

"We wanted everyone to fully understand that the Susan Caldwell Hospital of Florida would have Christian music, programs, conversation, and anything else we thought we could use as a witness tool to win someone over to Christ—on a daily basis. No one would be excluded from anything that was offered at the hospital. It was a lofty goal, but it wasn't a problem for the staff, volunteers, or patients. The potential problem was with patients who came in or were brought in for emergencies.

"Valarie is no quitter. She will stand her ground and not relinquish one spot until she gets what she wants."

Wherefore take unto you the whole armour of God, that ye may be able to withstand in the evil day, and having done all, to stand (Ephesians 6:13).

"If I didn't know any better, I would believe God put that scripture in especially for her. Of course I know He didn't, but you know what I mean.

"Since the hospital didn't have any government funding or grants, that wasn't an issue. The big issue for the government and city officials was patients that were admitted involuntarily—and in most cases unconscious. They said that we couldn't force our religion on anyone— under any circumstances. Our stand was that this wasn't a religion—and we should be able to express our faith anywhere and however we choose in an effort to be witnesses for Christ. By including in the bylaws that we would use whatever measure possible to be a witness for Jesus Christ in the administration of how our hospitals were run, patients would know beforehand.

"If a patient was brought to our hospitals by an emergency vehicle and later decided that he or she did not want to stay, he or she could transfer to another hospital at our expense. We were so confident that this would not happen too often that we were willing to take on the expense of transferring a patient if it did. After much prayer, deliberation, and the grace of God, we were successful. As you can see, the hospitals are up and running."

REFLECTIONS

A s this part of the interview was about to come to an end, Abraham asked me to allow him to reminisce for a moment.

"Maurice, it has been some time now since Valarie went home to be with the Lord, but I really thank God for the years we spent together. At times like this, I think about the joys, challenges, and victories we shared. I loved that woman so much, and she was so good to me that just thinking about her makes my heart skip a beat. Only God could influence our lives the way he did. I really miss her at times, but I know I will see her again in heaven."

"Maurice, as I sit here, I can truly say that God is faithful. God has truly done—and is doing—what He has promised. I find no fault in Him. In fact, if there is any fault or error, it is on my part. To see how God brought Valarie and me together—two people with different backgrounds and, in spite of ourselves, produced what He did—is amazing. I wouldn't trade what God has done for me with her for anything in this world. I'm what you would call a seasoned man—a person well over one hundred years old—but I know God is not finished with me yet. I know there is still something he wants me to do because, if that were not the case, I would be in heaven with Jesus instead of still here. Now is the time some folks might call my golden years, when I should just sit back and relax. Well, you know what? That sounds good, and, if it were not for the fact that God is stirring up in me to do something else, I would do just that. Thinking about where God has brought me from and what He has brought me through—yes, challenges and all—I cannot just sit by the wayside and do nothing.

"It has been said what does not kill you will make you stronger. I don't know about the killing part, but my faith in God has certainly been strengthened over the years. God is—and always will be—the answer. You can search, research, study, challenge, and even live, but—after all is said and done—God is still the answer. God loves you with such an unconditional love that he sent Jesus to pay the price to reconcile you back to Him to prove that love. Trust Him, love Him, lean on Him, and depend on Him. As you do that, you will find He is faithful and will never let you down."

"Maurice, you have my life story. If I left anything of importance out, it is because God wanted me to. It has been a pleasure spending this time with you. I trust you have enjoyed it as much as I have."

"I have had a nice time, Abraham," I said. "Listening to you tell your story let me know that the life you have lived—and is still living—is interesting and rewarding."

"Maurice, I know you are a young, upstart writer, but tell me: what goals are you trying to accomplish?"

I was surprised by the question, but I didn't have to search for an answer. "Y-y-you know what, Abraham? I would like t-t-to continue to write, but I would also like to have my own publishing outlet and u-u-use it primarily to help unknown writers get their material published. It is really a struggle to get your material published if y-yyou are not already established."

"I understand," Abraham said as he nodded his head. "Since we have been meeting, I have sought the Lord in what to do concerning you, and He told me to give you this gift. Do not open it now," he said, handing me an envelope. "I also want you to know that God instructed me to have all my book proceeds go to you—and that is what I will do."

Shocked, I said, "Abraham, y-y-you don't have to do that. I am sure what's in th-th-this envelope is plenty."

"Maurice, look around. As you can see, I have been blessed mightily because when God tells me to do something, I do it. So hush, the matter is closed."

As I was getting ready to leave, Abraham stopped me and said, "Maurice, if you don't mind, I would like to pray for you before you leave."

"Of course, I wouldn't mind that at all," I said.

I have been to churches and heard people pray, but I had never heard anyone pray with an authority like Abraham's, especially concerning myself.

"Heavenly Father, in the name of Jesus, I come to you giving you all praise, honor, and glory because you alone are worthy. I thank you that you are God all by yourself and there is none like you. I thank you for Jesus coming here on earth and fulfilling the purpose for which he came. Jesus proved Your and His amazing and unselfish love for all mankind by being the ultimate sacrifice, which was the price he had to pay for our salvation. Dear Father, I thank you for the Holy Spirit and how He is our Helper, Comforter, and guides us into all truth. Now Father, as I intercede on the behalf of Maurice, I would like to thank you for the purpose you have for his life. I thank you for the time we have spent together, and I trust I have been able to impart some of the anointing that is on my life into his.

"I thank you for watching over him as he continues to seek your will for his life, and I trust that he will walk with boldness that only you can give—walk in the fullness of what you have ordained for him. I pray that your presence and anointing will rise up in him to the measure that he will from this moment forward never be the same. I ask you, Father, to cause the fire of the Holy Spirit to become an internal inferno in him, causing him to have a desire and hunger for you like never before.

"Satan, right now, in the name of Jesus, I take authority over every plot, plan, or attack that you have orchestrated pertaining to Maurice's life. Satan, you have no right or authority! You are violating God's purpose for Maurice. I bind you according to God's word where it is written that whatsoever I loose on earth is loosed in heaven and whatsoever I bind on earth is bound in heaven. Satan, I remind you that no weapon formed against Maurice will prosper. Stuttering is a name and every name has to bow to the name of Jesus. Stuttering, I break the hold you have on Maurice's speech and command you to release him in the mighty name of Jesus.

"Heavenly Father, I thank you that Maurice is an overcomer and more than a conqueror in Jesus Christ. Lord Jesus, you said you confirm your word with signs following. I thank you for confirming your word as it pertains to victory in every area of Maurice's life, whether it is spiritual, physical, mental, social, or financial. Heavenly Father, I know you hear me when I pray, and I know because you hear me that you grant me the petition I lay before you. I thank you for this and all things. I pray in the name of Jesus Christ. Amen."

After praying, we hugged, and Abraham said, "Maurice, I perceive that you are a man with a good heart and try to do what's right. I would like for you to promise me something."

"Anything, Abraham. What is it?"

"I want you to promise that you will remember that whatever God gives you is not for you to hoard for yourself—you are to use it to bless others so they can see God's goodness. This promise is no more than what God told the children of Israel in the following scripture:

> But thou shalt remember the
> Lord Thy God: for it is he that
> Giveth Thee power to get wealth,
> That he may establish his covenant
> Which he sware unto thy fathers, as
> It is this day (Deuteronomy 8:18).

When I got home, I opened the envelope and found a check written out to me for $2.5 million. I was so elated that I just cried.

That was more than fifteen years ago. Since then, I have married and have a beautiful four-year-old. When my daughter was born, I was so excited that I couldn't stop spreading the news. God reminded me of the time when Abraham prayed for me about my stutter. I can't say exactly when I stopped, but I know that I have received the full manifestation of that prayer.

Abraham and I have had dinner a couple of times after our interviews, but I am usually busy concentrating on what God wants me to do and being a good steward over what He blessed me with.

I am grateful for what God has done for me through Abraham's ministry and will always cherish the time we spent together. As you can see, I have my own publishing firm—it is called Anyman's Publishing.

CONCLUSION

I want to reiterate this is a fictional story that could happen if you dare to believe God. Just like what developed when Abraham and Maurice's lives intertwined, something of that nature or even greater can happen in our lives. As we listen and obey God when he tells us what to do, and bless those individuals we encounter, expect the impossible.

> Be not forgetful to entertain
> Strangers: for thereby some
> Have entertained angels
> Unawares (Hebrews 13:2).

I pray that by reading this book, God's blessings will overtake you and His grace will empower you to the magnitude that—as you welcome people into your world—your life and their lives will be changed far more than you could have imagined.

God bless you and may His light shine on you forever.

About the Author

Daniel Leviston is the founder and president of Daniel Leviston Ministries. He is an evangelist who preaches and teaches the uncompromised word of God. A freelance writer, Daniel, his beautiful wife, Rena, and their lovely daughter, Autumn, reside in Gainesville, Florida.